gnu

cheetah

crocodile

hippo

ostrich

pelican

zebra

weaver

Andrea Schütze tried out almost any hobby you can think of when she was a child. At some point she decided to stick with reading which is why she enjoys writing books so much. She is a trained women's tailor and has earned a degree in psychology, however, she never received a basic level swimming certificate. This picture book was created thanks to a question.

Tina Nagel, born in 1977, studied graphic design with a focus on book design and illustration in Trier, Germany. She has been working as a freelance graphic designer and illustrator since 2004.

For Rosalie
This is my answer.
A.S.

PLURUS BOOKS
ISBN : 9781910271155
© 2014
An Imprint of Wimbledon Publishing Company Limited
75-76 Blackfriars Road, London SE1 8HA
Ich bleib immer bei dir
© ellermann im Dressler Verlag, Hamburg 2013.

Andrea Schütze · Tina Nagel

I WILL ALWAYS STAY WITH YOU

PLURUS BOOKS

Far away behind the hills, the sun is about to set. Mummy elephant and the little elephant lie down close to the big tree to go to sleep.

Tired, the little elephant huddles against mummy's soft trunk and covers himself with her big ears. Mummy elephant kisses the little elephant good night and whispers softly, 'Sleep well, little one, and sweet dreams.' Then she closes her eyes and starts to snore, softly.

The little elephant is feeling warm and safe, but there is still something he can't get off his mind.

After a while he whispers directly into mummy's ear:
'Mummy, for how much longer can I actually stay with you?'
Mummy elephant lifts her eyelids and says, 'Until you are grown-up.'
'And when is that?' asks the little elephant.
'That is still a looong time away!' says Mummy elephant with a yawn.

The little elephant is quiet for a while.
Then he asks, 'Yes, but how long is long?'
Mummy elephant looks at her little
elephant, smiles and says:

'Long is as long as it takes for the zebras to paint zebra stripes on all the animals.'
'Oh, but that's fast!' says the little elephant. 'Isn't there something that takes longer?'

'Long is as long as it takes Daddy elephant to empty the whole lake there,' says Mummy elephant.

'Well,' says the little elephant, chuckling. 'If Daddy's really thirsty, that's fast. Say something that takes even longer!'

'As long is as long as it takes the snail to creep around the world.'
'Even looonger!' says little elephant.

'As long as it takes a desert bird to peck a cave into the rocks,' says Mummy elephant.
'A cave just for himself?' asks little elephant and stares at the tiny bird.

'Why, no,' says Mummy elephant. 'So huge that all the animals of the world could live there.'
Still, little elephant insists, 'Much, much longer.'

'You can stay with me for
as long as it takes the ants
to build a hill that reaches the moon.'

'Muuuch longer than even that,'
says little elephant.

'Hmm…' Mummy elephant is thinking. 'For as long as giraffes will have long necks,' she says.
'Much, much longer than that,' says little elephant.

'For as long as there won't be snow in the desert,' says Mummy elephant. 'Brr…!' The little elephant huddles closer against his Mummy. 'And now say the longest you can think of, Mummy!' Mummy elephant takes some time to think.

'For as long as it takes these seeds to become trees,' she says and gently covers a couple of seeds with soil. 'And for these trees to become a forest,' says little elephant happily. 'Yes! That takes pretty long!'

'But do you know what is the longest of all?' asks Mummy elephant. Little elephant shakes his head.
'Are you quite sure that you want to know what is the longest of all?' asks Mummy elephant.
The little elephant nods, eagerly.

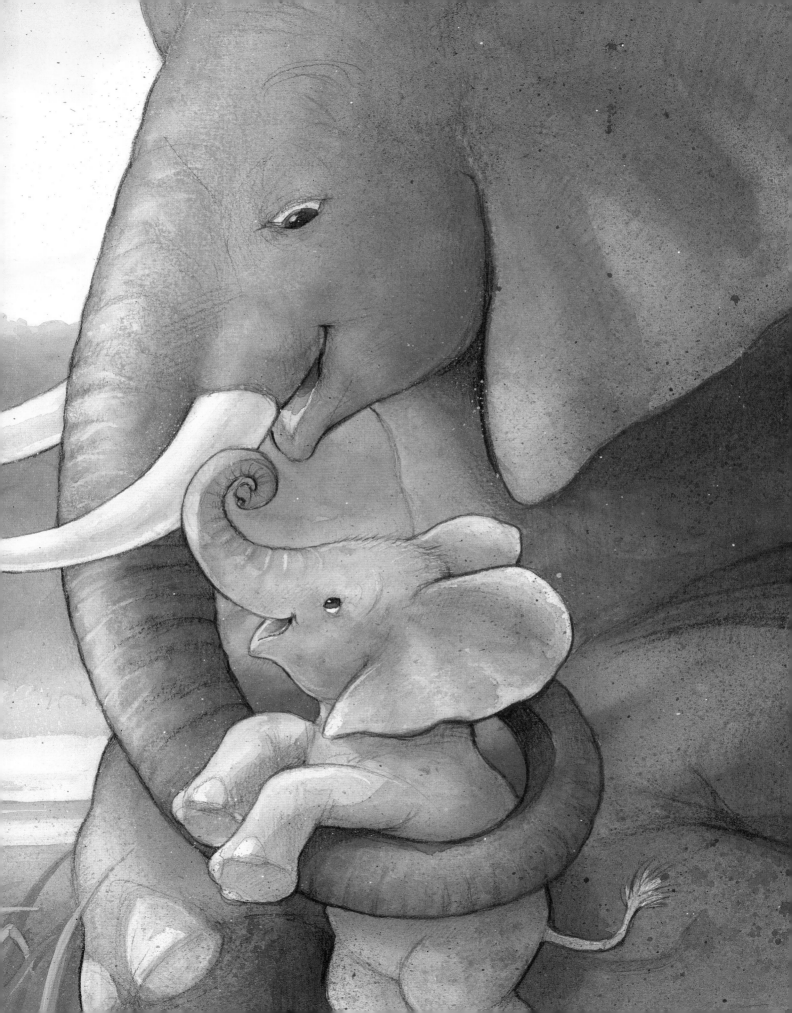

'You can stay with me for as long as you want!'
Then she closes her eyes again and falls asleep.
'As long as I want!' the little elephant whispers, happily.
'That really is very, very long!'

antelope

lion

ant

rhino

giraffe

bush squirrel

elephant